the BAD GUYS

EPISODE

6

ALIEN VS
BAD GUYS

A SCHOLASTIC PRESS BOOK
FROM SCHOLASTIC AUSTRALIA

SCHOLASTIC PRESS
345 PACIFIC HIGHWAY LINDFIELD NSW 2070
AN IMPRINT OF SCHOLASTIC AUSTRALIA PTY LIMITED
(ABN 11 000 614 577)
PO BOX 579 GOSFORD NSW 2250
WWW.SCHOLASTIC.COM.AU

PART OF THE SCHOLASTIC GROUP
SYDNEY • AUCKLAND • NEW YORK • TORONTO • LONDON • MEXICO CITY
• NEW DELHI • HONG KONG • BUENOS AIRES • PUERTO RICO

FIRST PUBLISHED BY SCHOLASTIC AUSTRALIA IN 2017.
TEXT AND ILLUSTRATIONS COPYRIGHT © AARON BLABEY, 2017.

NATIONAL LIBRARY OF AUSTRALIA CATALOGUING-IN-PUBLICATION ENTRY
CREATOR: BLABEY, AARON, AUTHOR.
TITLE: THE BAD GUYS EPISODE 6 / AARON BLABEY.
ISBN: 978-1-76027-948-6 (PAPERBACK)
SERIES: BLABEY, AARON. BAD GUYS; BK. 6.
TARGET AUDIENCE: FOR PRIMARY SCHOOL AGE.
SUBJECTS: AUSTRALIAN FICTION.
CHILDREN'S STORIES.

TYPESET IN JANSON, ELO, KERBEROS FANG AND BEHANCE.
DESIGN BY NICOLE STOFBERG.

PRINTED IN AUSTRALIA BY GRIFFIN PRESS.
SCHOLASTIC AUSTRALIA'S POLICY, IN ASSOCIATION WITH GRIFFIN PRESS,
IS TO USE PAPERS THAT ARE RENEWABLE AND MADE EFFICIENTLY
FROM WOOD GROWN IN RESPONSIBLY MANAGED FORESTS,
SO AS TO MINIMISE ITS ENVIRONMENTAL FOOTPRINT.

17 18 19 20 21 / 1

· AARON BLABEY ·

the BAD GUYS

EPISODE

6

ALIEN VS
BAD GUYS

GOOD GUYS CLUB SAVES THE WORLD!

There are celebrations across the globe tonight, as the evil **DR RUPERT MARMALADE** has been **DEFEATED!**

TIFFANY FLUFFIT 6

Yes, that's right—every kitten, puppy, bunny, pony and dolphin has been turned from a

FLESH-EATING ZOMBIE BACK into our cute and furry friends!

And **WHO** do we have to thank?

6

THE GOOD GUYS CLUB!

AS GOOD AS IT GETS!

Sure, the name might be lame, but I doubt there's a creature on this planet that wouldn't like to give those

CHEEKY, WHOLESOME BOYS

a hug!

3

The **LOVABLE**
Mr Wolf!

The **BRILLIANT**
Mr Snake!

The **POWERFUL**
Mr Shark!

And
THE OTHER ONE
that is some kind of fish.
Possibly a sardine.

They are the
GREATEST LEGENDS OF OUR TIME!

ARTIST'S IMPRESSION

And I'd personally like to add that I **ALWAYS** thought they were awesome.

I really did . . .

So let's send them all a great, big . . .

THANK YOU, wherever they may be!

To the gang that saved the world—

NOT BAD, GUYS ... not bad at all!

It's nice to think of you out there ...

wherever you are . . .

protecting us . . .

you GREAT, BIG, BEAUTIFUL TOUGH GUYS . . .

· CHAPTER 1 ·
DEEP SPACE, DEEP POO

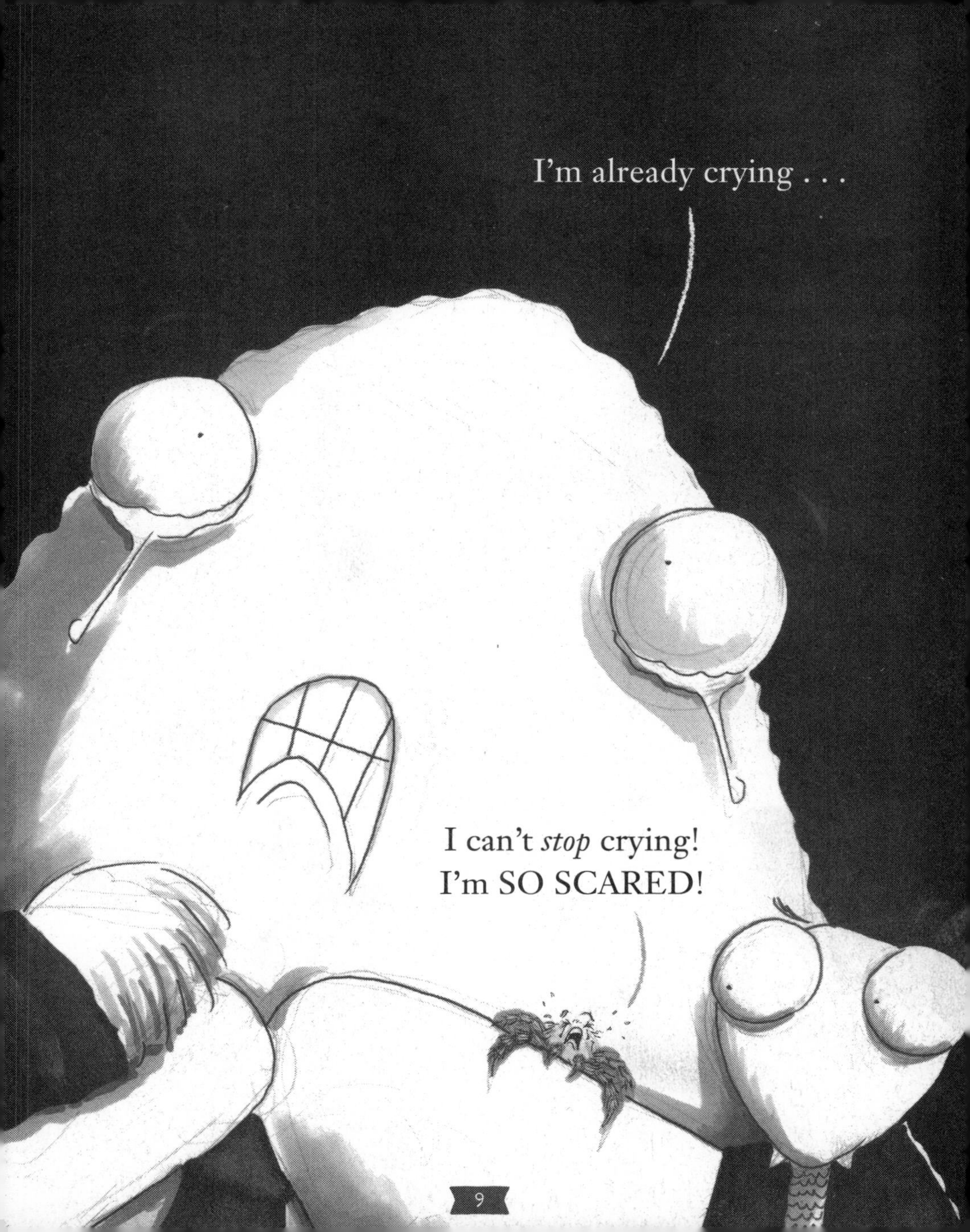
I'm already crying . . .
I can't *stop* crying!
I'm SO SCARED!

Pull yourselves together, will you?
WE HAVE TO GET OUT OF HERE!

How?! **HE'S AN ALIEN!**
Marmalade **ISN'T** a guinea pig.
He's an enormous hostile alien life-form with
MORE TEETH, TENTACLES
and **BUTTS** than any decent creature
should have . . .

And we're trapped inside its space station on the moon **WITHOUT A ROCKET.**

So **HOW ARE WE GOING TO GET OUT OF HERE?!**

Shhh! It'll hear us! What are we going to do? We can't hide here forever . . .

SPLODGE!

Eeeeee!
Nobody
move . . .

Wait!
It's moving away!
LOOK AT ALL THAT GOO!

SPLODGE!

SPLODGE!

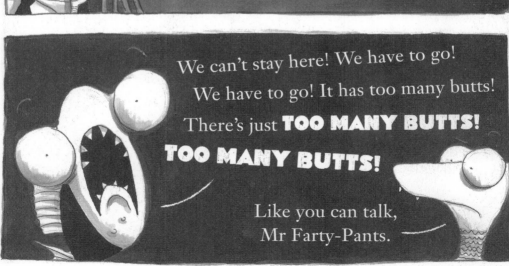

We can't stay here! We have to go!
We have to go! It has too many butts!
There's just **TOO MANY BUTTS!**
TOO MANY BUTTS!

Like you can talk,
Mr Farty-Pants.

Oh man, this is SO not fair.
We've come so far!
Finally, everyone thinks we're
heroes! We can't die here.
We need a plan . . .

Hey! What's *that*?

Legs!
*Where are
you going?!*

SCUTTLE!

SCUTTLE!

SCUTTLE!

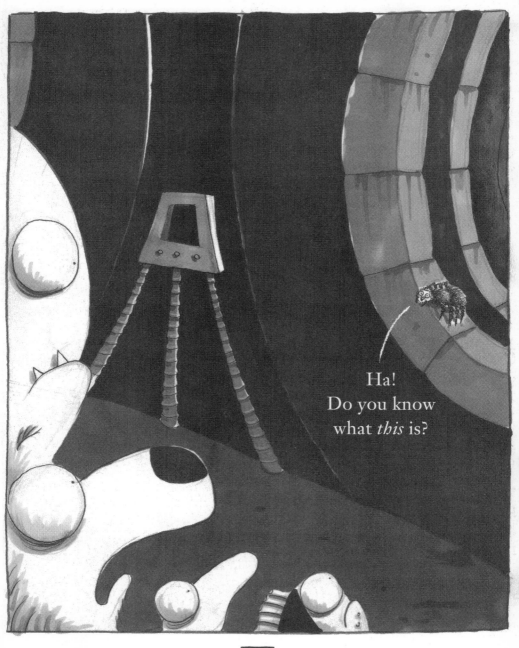

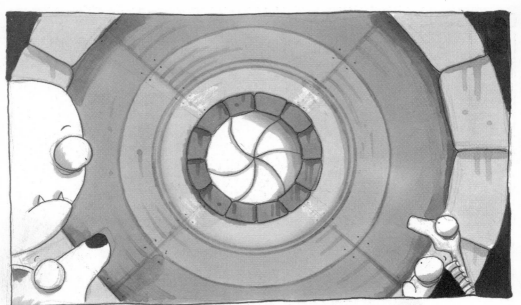

Is it the little room where we all die?

But this is an
ALIEN SPACESHIP!
How will you even know how to work it?

How hard can it be? I bet there are a whole **BUNCH OF LANGUAGES** on here and probably some from **EARTH** and . . . yep . . . and what if I just punch in a few **CO-ORDINATES** and . . . yep . . .

ready to launch

destination > earth

I'd say we're good to go!

Man, you just **HACKED AN ALIEN COMPUTER!** Seriously, we don't give you as much credit as you deserve. Let's hear it for Legs, guys!

OK, I'll tell you what— why don't you stay here and **HAVE A PARADE FOR LEGS** and I'll see you back on Earth. OK?

You are the rudest little—

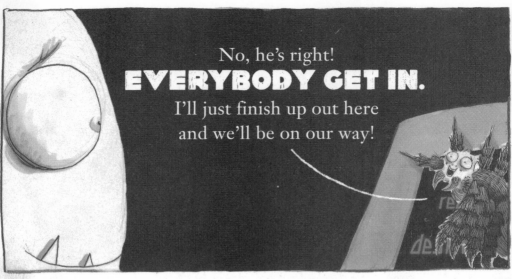

And you're right, Mr Shark . . .

FOOMP!

Seriously, what would we do without Legs?

In fact, how's it going out there, little buddy?

Legs? Is everything cool?

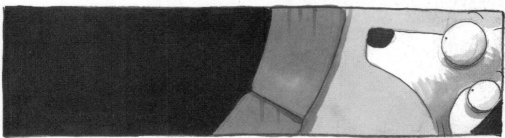

LEGS?!

· CHAPTER 2 ·
AND THEN THERE WERE FOUR

Are you serious?

YEAH!

I mean, there's **PLENTY** of these pod things. Legs can just take the **NEXT ONE**. He's probably just gone to **GRAB A SANDWICH** or something and I'm sure he wouldn't mind if we took off and met him back on—

NO-ONE LEAVES UNTIL WE FIND LEGS. GOT IT?

I mean, yeah, we **COULD** do that, but don't you think it makes more sense to—

WHAT ARE YOU TALKING ABOUT?!

LEGS IS OUR **FRIEND!**

HE'S THE **ONLY REASON** WE KNOW ABOUT THE ESCAPE PODS IN THE FIRST PLACE AND **YOU WANT TO LEAVE HIM BEHIND?!**

Hey, Piranha! Keep it down!

NO! I'VE HAD IT UP TO HERE WITH THIS ROTTEN LITTLE DIABLO!

I'm just **SAYING**—I think Legs would **WANT** us to save—

YOU ARE THE MOST SELFISH . . .

Piranha!

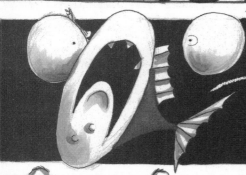

MEAN-HEARTED . . .

Really, man—*shoosh!*

SON OF A WORM I'VE EVER . . . .

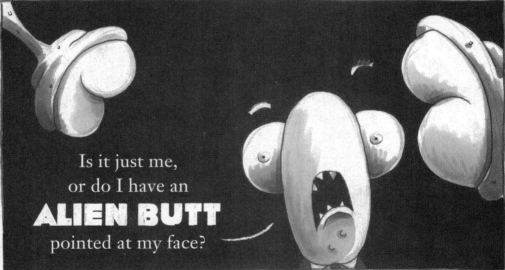

Is it just me,
or do I have an

ALIEN BUTT

pointed at my face?

Piranha! *Look out!*

Oh my stars!
It uses its
BUTTS AS HANDS!

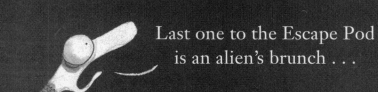

What **ARE YOU SAYING?!** That thing has **BUTT HANDS!** You really want to go looking for a creature with great, big **POOPY BUTT HANDS?!**

Shut up and listen!

TOOOOOOOOOO MAANNNYYYYY!

BUUUUUTTTTTSSSSSSSSSS!!!

He's still ALIVE!
We can follow his voice!

Let's go!

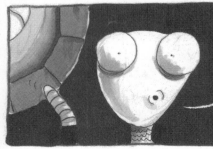

But what about the Escape Pod?
Maybe I should just stay here
and look after it, in case . . .

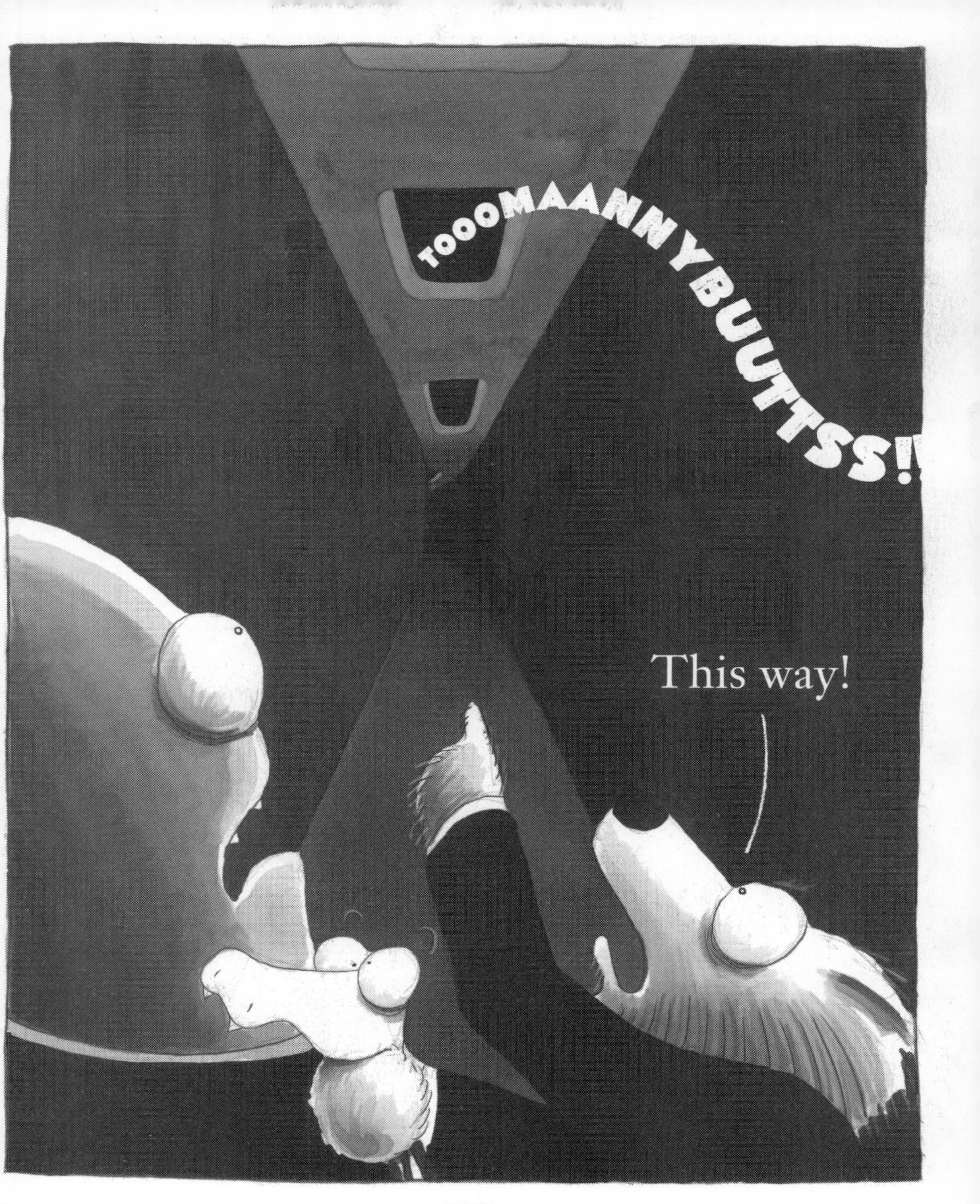
TOOOMAAANNYBUUTTSS!!
This way!

· CHAPTER 3 ·
THE LADY ALIEN

OK, if you vote to stop looking for our friends, raise your hands.

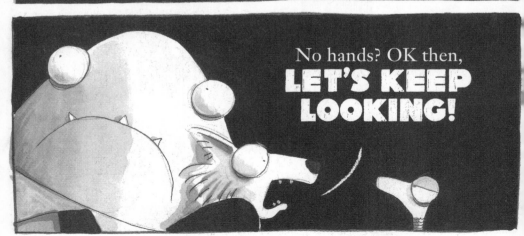

No hands? OK then, **LET'S KEEP LOOKING!**

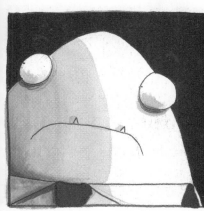

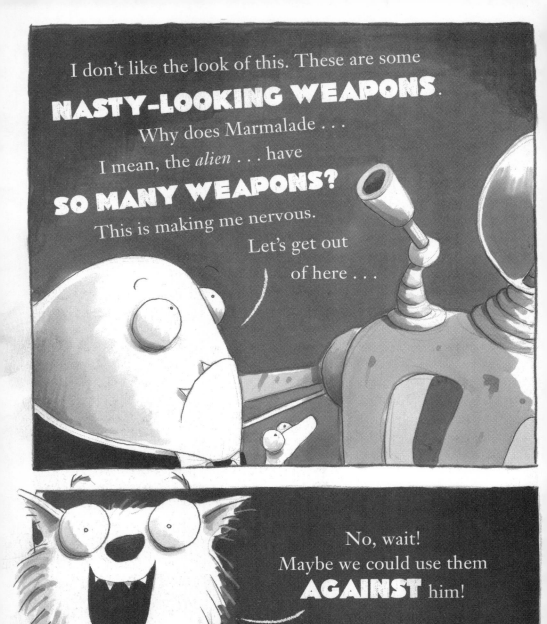

Oh really? And you're trained in using **BIZARRE ALIEN WEAPONS**, are you?

No, but maybe we could figure it out.

FIGURE IT OUT?!
OK, well why don't you take a few minutes to learn how to

SPEAK ALIEN

and then—have a flick through the

INSTRUCTION MANUALS

and then—mosey on over and TEACH US how to use them too! Yeah. GREAT idea. Let's just all take a seat and

FIGURE IT OUT!

No! Snake!

Don't interrupt me, man!
You need to hear this—

SNAKE!
IT'S HERE!
AARRGGHHH!!!

SHARK?!
Man, you are SO
good at disguises.

I know.

But how did you manage
to make this so quickly?

I'm just good at it.
Let it go.

What's with the **DRESS?!**

I'm going to pretend to be a **LADY ALIEN**. And when the **MARMALADE ALIEN** tries to make friends with me, I'll get him to show us where he keeps the creatures that he's captured and **BINGO**— we can rescue the guys. **THAT'S** the plan.

OK, your costumes may have worked in the past, but what you just said is so stupid it makes me want to eat my own face.

Well, I like it.

IT'S INSANE!

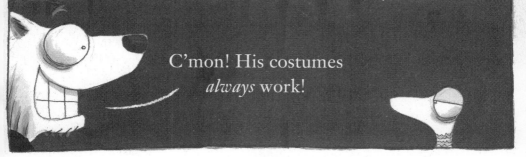

C'mon! His costumes *always* work!

Yeah, Snake.
It'll work! I mean,

LOOK!

This tentacle is
SO realistic!
Seriously
Shark, it's . . .

. . . how did you make it
look . . . so . . . *real?*

· CHAPTER 4 ·
ROUND IN CIRCLES

It's so dark.
Why is it so dark?
It seems to be
getting darker . . .
Don't you think it's
REALLY dark?

YES! WELL SPOTTED! IT'S DARK!
WHAT DO YOU WANT?
A *COOKIE*?
OBVIOUSLY, IT'S DARK.

Give me a break!
I'm **TERRIFIED**!
Everyone's gone. Even Shark!
But we can't give up! If we just
keep searching I **KNOW**
we'll find them. We're getting
CLOSE, I can feel it.

Oh really? We're getting *close*?
Then how do you explain **THIS** . . .

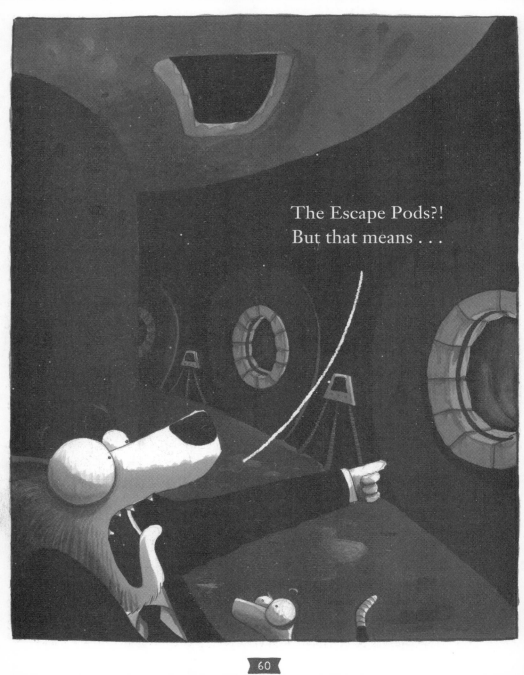

It **MEANS** we've been **WALKING AROUND IN CIRCLES**.

Listen to me, Wolf . . .

I'll admit it, **PART OF ME** really does want to be a hero. It's true. Part of me really, *really* does. But you know what I've learnt from following you around on all these stupid missions? Do you know what I've learnt from every ridiculous situation you've put us in? **DO YOU?**

I've learnt I'm *not* a hero.
I know you want me to be one . . .

But I'm really, really not.

I know **YOU** want to be a hero.
And who knows—
MAYBE YOU ARE.
But I also think that you're **CRAZY**.
And I think, one day, you'll make
just one too many stupid decisions
and you **WILL** go and get
yourself eaten by an alien.
And Wolf?

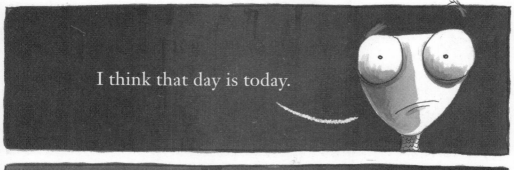

I think that day is today.

I've never had a friend before, Wolf. And even though I do call you an idiot quite a lot . . . I know that you're the best friend I'll ever have. And I don't want to lose you. So . . .

Please get in the Escape Pod with me.

You know I can't, Mr Snake.

And you know why, too.

I can't **MAKE** you do anything, buddy. What you do next is up to you. There's the **ESCAPE POD**. If you really want to leave, then go ahead, get in and go. But I have a feeling that you'll do the right—

WHAT?!
I didn't think you'd
actually get in!

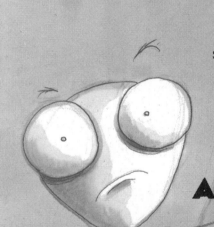

Why? Because of my little
speech? Well yeah, I meant it
and everything but there's an

**ALIEN WITH
BUTT-HANDS**
out there so basically,
ALL BETS ARE OFF
and—

What?

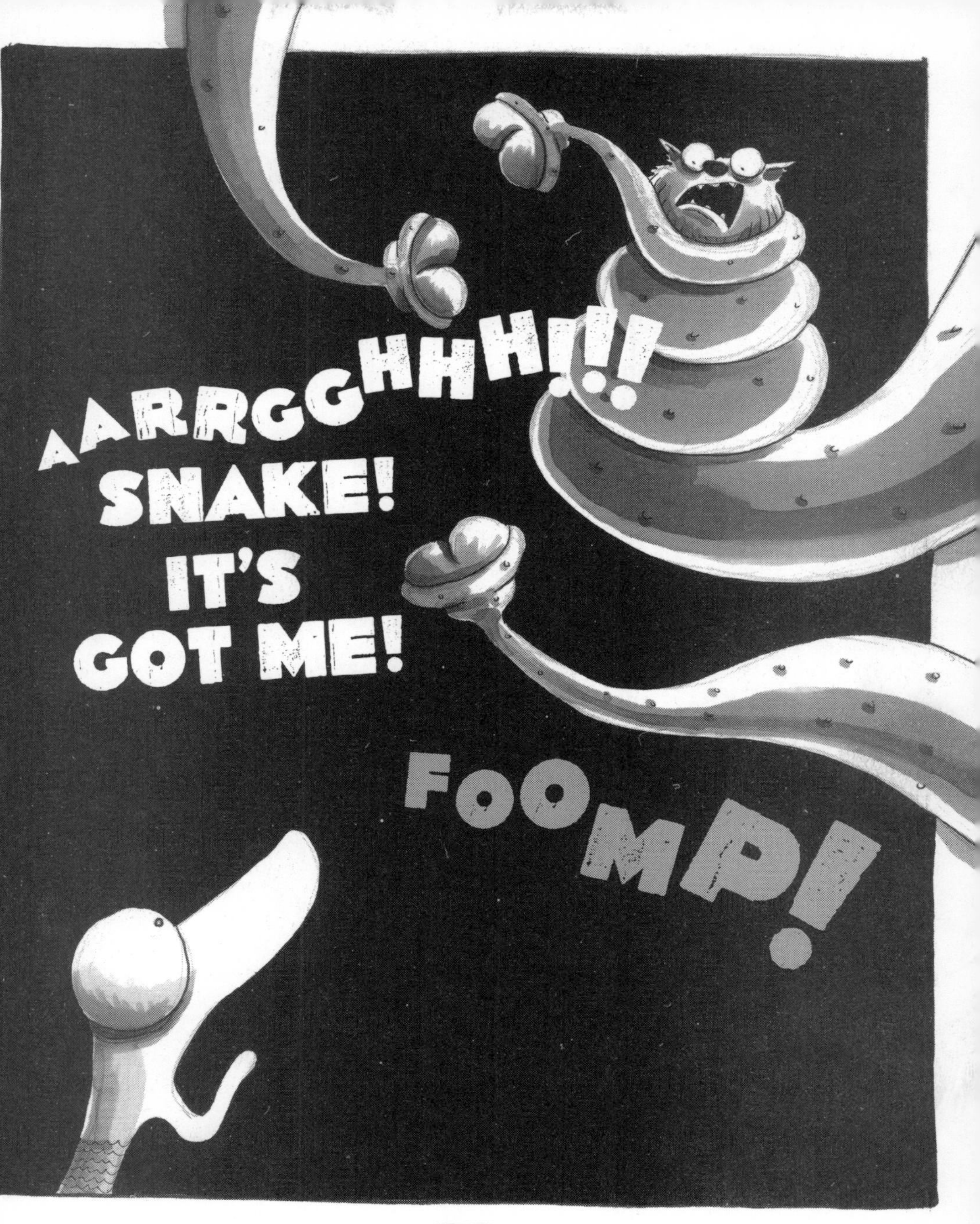
AARRGGHHHH!!!
SNAKE!
IT'S
GOT ME!
FOOMP!

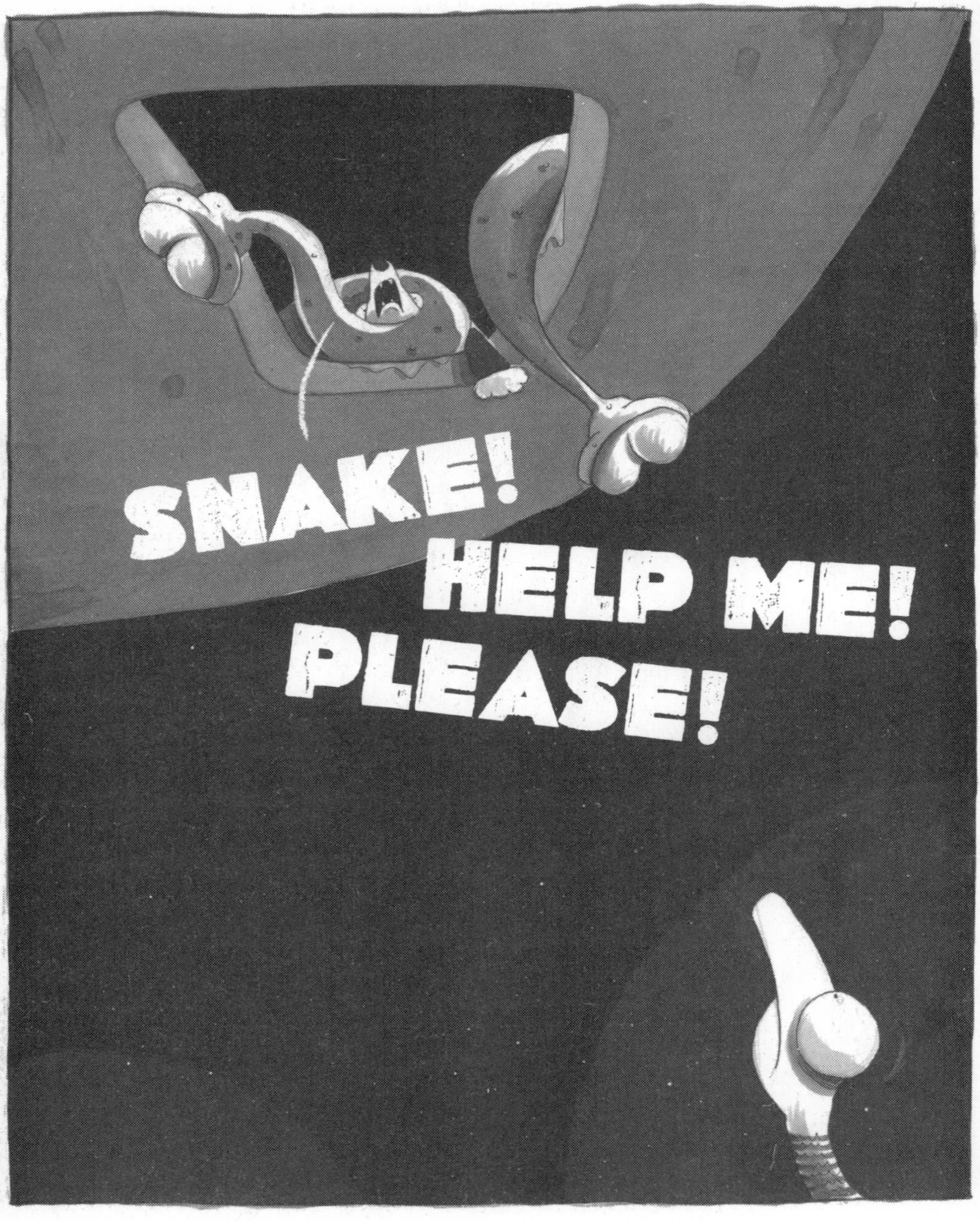
SNAKE!
HELP ME!
PLEASE!

· CHAPTER 5 ·
THE PIT OF DOOM

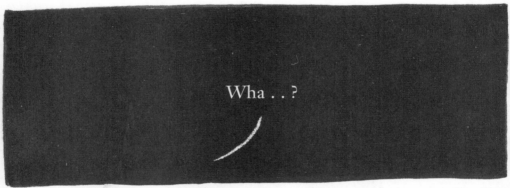

Wha . . ?

I can't move!

Yeah, it's **DRIED SNOT**.
It came out of the alien's nose holes.

Shark!

Well, considering how
many butts it has, I
suppose we should be
grateful it's just snot.

Legs!

Hey Wolfie. I've got to be honest—we were kind of hoping next time we saw you, you'd be **RESCUING US**.

It's true. We're pleased to see you, but I think we're all pretty disappointed, too.

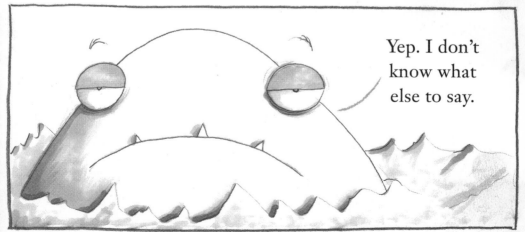

Yep. I don't know what else to say.

Don't worry, guys! I think you're forgetting something . . .

Mr Snake!

Is that meant to be funny?

LET ME
SHOW YOU...

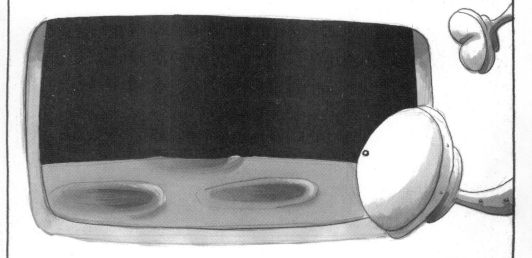

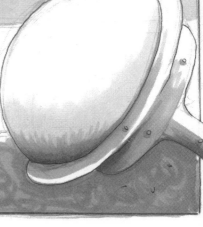

What a surprise.

Yeah. What a shocker.

I can't believe he left us . . .

REALLY?! YOU ACTUALLY **CAN'T** BELIEVE IT?!

· CHAPTER 6 ·
THE END OF THE ROAD

Hey you! Butt-hands!
When you **FART**,
is it from a single tentacle
or do all the disgusting
things go off at once?

WELL, I'M NOT SURE, LITTLE FISHY....

LET'S FIND OUT!

Oh man, I didn't think that through . . .

Hey Marmalade! Why did you pretend to be a **GUINEA PIG?** What was the point of that?

WELL, NO-ONE TAKES MUCH NOTICE OF SILLY LITTLE GUINEA PIGS. SO I WAS ABLE TO STUDY YOUR PLANET VERY CAREFULLY WITHOUT ANYBODY NOTICING . . .

And what did you learn?

APART FROM THE FACT THAT PIRANHAS AND SHARKS DON'T NEED TO BE IN WATER AS MUCH AS YOU'D THINK?

Yeah. Apart from that . . .

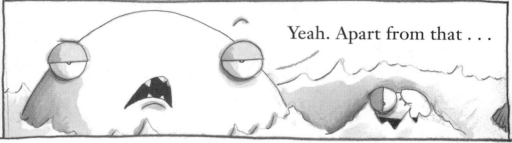

I LEARNT THAT YOUR PLANET IS HELPLESS.

AND IT WILL BE MINE.

I feel so stupid. I thought you were doing all of this just because you didn't like being **CUTE** and **CUDDLY**.

Oh, that wasn't a lie.
On my planet, **I AM** cute and cuddly.
And **I HATE** it. Don't get me started.

Is your name even 'Marmalade'?

YOU COULDN'T PRONOUNCE MY REAL NAME, WOLF.

Try me.

My name is **KDJFLOERHGCOINWERUHCG LEIRWFHEKLWJFHXALHW.**

Yeah.
Well,
whatevs.

What do you want with us,
KDJFLOERHGCOINWERUHCG LEIRWFHEKLWJFHXALHW?

Yeah, yeah. That sounds great, KDJFdddd—whatever, and yeah, we all saw your weird, creepy **WEAPONS**, but you know what? You don't stand a chance!

OH REALLY? AND WHY'S THAT?

Because there's only **ONE** of you and you're no match for **AGENT FOX** and the **INTERNATIONAL LEAGUE OF HEROES!**

HMMM. THAT FOX IS VERY CLEVER...

BUT, GUESS WHAT?

IT'S NOT JUST ME! THERE ARE THOUSANDS OF US . . .

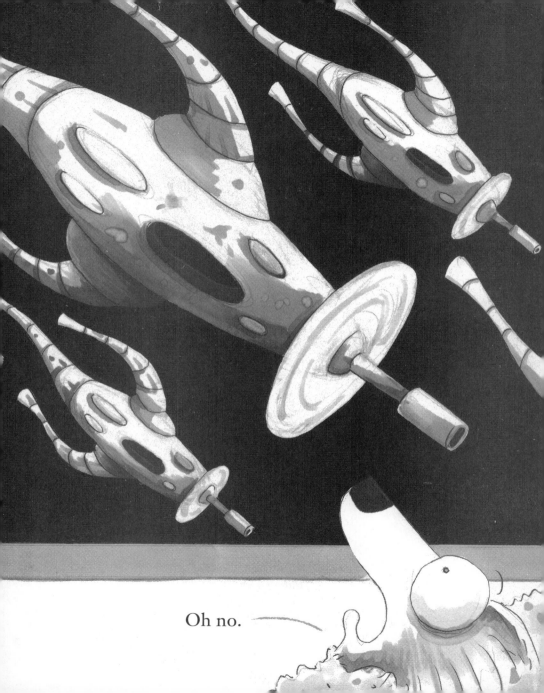

Oh no.

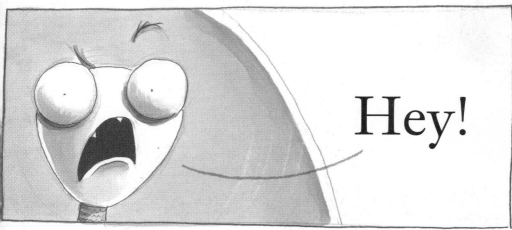

· CHAPTER 7 ·
PICK ON SOMEONE YOUR OWN SIZE

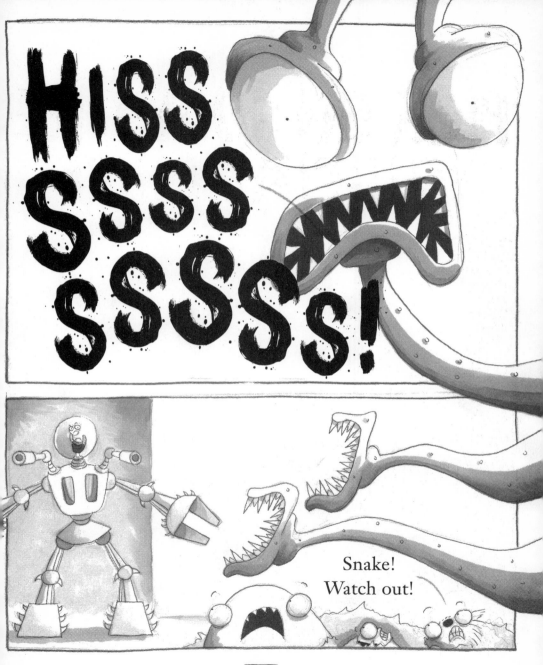

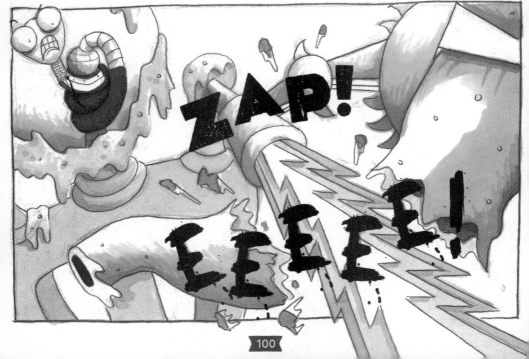

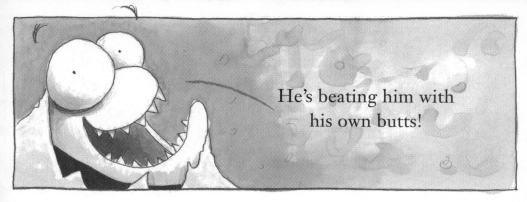

He's beating him with his own butts!

EVERYONE, HOLD ONTO SOMETHING!

DANGER!
OUTER DOOR

CLUNK!

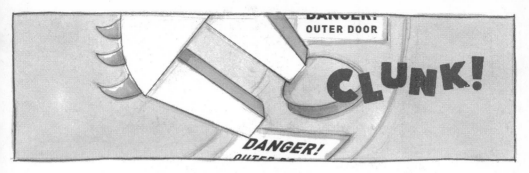

You did it, Snake!

YOU CAME BACK!

YOU CAME BACK!

What changed your mind?

I guess I just finally got sick of being a Bad Guy.

Hey Chicos!

As much as I want to dance my dance

of joy right now, there's a whole

ALIEN ARMY OUT THERE WAITING TO DESTROY EARTH!

We need to get home and warn **AGENT FOX.**

You're right. Let's get out of here, guys. But the good news is—this alien army doesn't have a **LEADER** anymore, thanks to YOU, Mr Snake!

VOOMP!

AND MY FRIENDS LET ME BACK IN.

Wait a minute!

Did you just call him **KDJFLOER HGCOINWERU HCGLEIRWFHEK LWJFHXALHW?!**

GET THEM!

· CHAPTER 8 ·
THE POD

I'm sorry, Legs, I had to fire off the first Pod to **TRICK** Marmalade. How long will it take you to prep another one?

I'll do it as fast as I can, Mr Hero!

Snake, I'm so proud of you! I mean . . . *how did you get that weapon thing to work?!*

I just . . . figured it out.

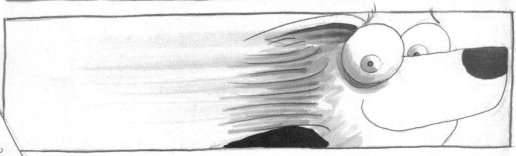

SNAP!

EEEEEEE! Oh man, they're everywhere!

Watch out!

That's it!

THE DRIBBLE!

Everyone—GET ON
MY BACK!

Now hold on **TIGHT.**

Legs, I hate to rush you but—

I'm on it . . .

I don't mind rushing you!

HURRY CHICO!

I'm on it!

Everyone get in!

Um . . .

Um *WHAT*?!

There's a setting here that kind of bothers me. I'm not sure what it means.

WHO CARES WHAT IT MEANS?!

JUST GET IN HERE AND SEND US BACK TO EARTH!

Yeah . . . OK . . .
I guess it'll be OK . . .

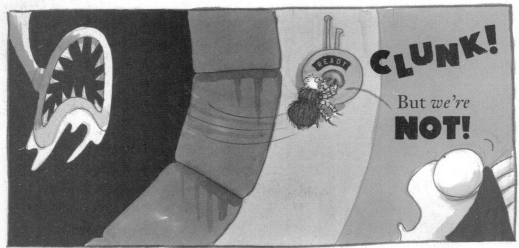

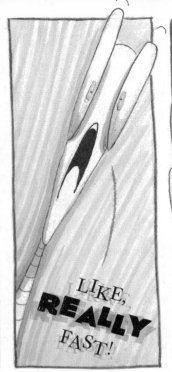

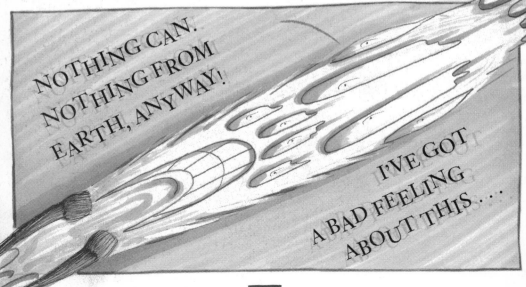

CHAPTER 9
OUT OF THE FRYING PAN, INTO THE...
HANG ON, THAT'S NOT INVENTED YET...

I can't lie, Chicos. I thought there'd be a bit of a crowd waiting to welcome us. I've got my Party Pants on . . .

Yeah. And we have to warn Agent Fox.

Where is everyone?

Maybe we're just in the **WRONG SPOT.**

Did we land in another country or something?

Ahhhh, no. As far as I can tell, we've landed right back where we arranged to **MEET AGENT FOX.**

What do you mean, Legs? We're in the **MIDDLE OF NOWHERE**. You must be reading that thing wrong.

Hmmm. I wish I was . . .

Don't stress, guys! We're home! That's the main thing. We're home, but this time it's *different*. This time we're **HEROES!**

Ohhhhh. Being heroes isn't the only thing that's different . . .

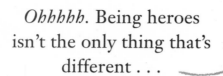

What do you mean, Legs?

Well, remember that setting that was bothering me? It seems . . . it was the control for a slightly

DIFFERENT KIND OF TRAVEL . . .

You mean that's
the thing that
made us go so
FAST?

Well, maybe . . . but that's
not what I mean . . .

Spit it out, Spider!
WHERE
ARE WE?!

Mr Snake, the question isn't
'WHERE' . . .

65 MILLION BC?! Are you kidding?! **65 MILLION BC?!** But that's when . . .

When what?

Oh my stars! You're right! That's when there were . . .

That's when there were **WHAT?!**

DINOS

TO BE CONTINUED . . .

IT'S ON.

EPISODE 7
COMING SOON!